HOPE for the FROGS

A story written by
Asa H. Sparks,

with pictures drawn by
JoAnn Dick,

published by

JALMAR Press, Inc.
Sacramento, California.

Published and distributed by
JALMAR Press, Inc.
6501 Elvas Avenue
Sacramento, CA 95819

ISBN 0-915190-17-6

Library of Congress: 78-72061

Printed in United States of America

Dedicated to:
Phil, Don, Charleigh,
Lori, Dean, Libbie,
Hilda, Dick, Sandy,
Winston, Andy, Robert,
Norma, Martha, Earline,
Maryann, Leif and Roy
Who helped me
feel less like a frog.
Asa Sparks

Freddie Frog wondered about the world all around him.

Early many mornings he watched the sun come up over his world. Reflected in the pond that seemed like an ocean, the sun brought light. He glowed under those sunrises.

In the evenings as the same sun showered beauty and peace from the mountainous hills in the distance, Freddie glimmered under the sunsets.

From five-star restaurants to mom's home cooking, he loved good food. He loved to share a cold coke with a friend.

6

Freddie kept up with the best sellers and the obscure little gems of writing.

He read and responded to many thoughts.

Although he watched and admired the athletes in the National Frogball League, and although he tried to out-jump every other frog in the pond,

there was a special and
sensitive side to Freddie.
He spent many hours
searching for the soft
and tender.

Freddie tried in every way he knew to be a prince...

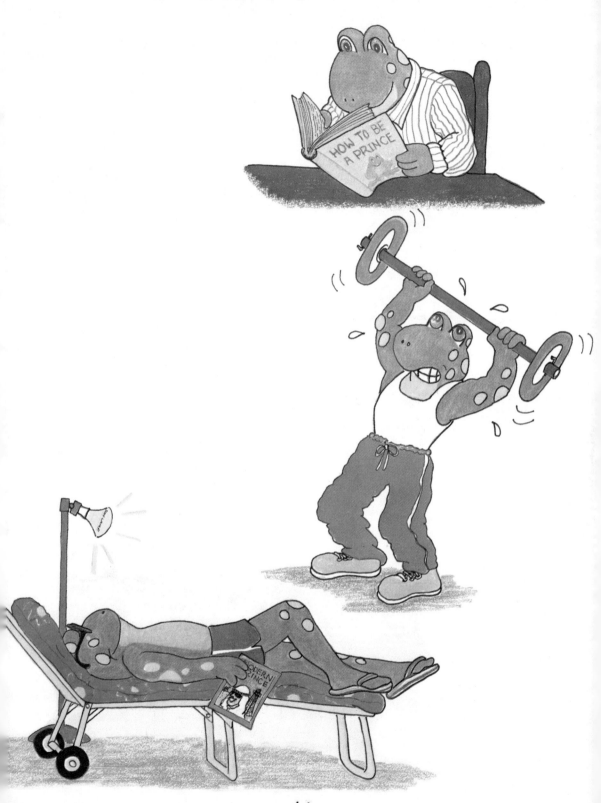

But no princess ever
looked at Freddie.

reddie bought a high-powered, low-slung sporty car with a hot engine and a cool set of seats.

All the princesses saw was the car.

None of them even glanced
at lonely Freddie.

15

Each year he saved money to go on cruises and watched moonlit nights over the waters without a princess by his side.

With hand-crafted boots from Italy, slacks from L.A., shirts from Paris and native jewelries,

Freddie wore the latest styles...

and everyone looked through him as though he were not there.

19

ALONE

Freddie walked the streets of his city while princes and princesses passed him by.

No one ever felt as lonely as Freddie.

He could hardly concentrate.

His work suffered.

and though he tried
steak or lobster or omelets,
meals were tasteless.
23

He tried rock and Rach-
maninoff, but concerts
became less and less fun.

More and more Freddie
resembled a frog, for
there was no princess to
kiss him and turn him
into a magical
prince.

And then one day,
Freddie met Libbie...
It could have
been
at work,

or school,

26

in church,

or in the
rain,

27

in an
elevator,

or on
a bus!

28

There is no magical place for frogs to meet a princess. Besides, Libbie was certainly not a princess.

Oh, she was OK, but certainly not a princess.

But they began talking
about weather and politics
and work and life...

and as they chatted on and
on, Freddie revealed more
and more about himself.
And for each thing he told
about himself, she told
something more  about
herself.

One night, Freddie dreamed of her dancing at a royal ball and wondered the next day...

..."Is Libbie a princess in disguise?"

33

More and more as together they talked and walked and worked and ate, he saw the princess she really was.

A strange thing was happening at the same time to Freddie. The more she responded to the princess Freddie saw, the more like a prince he felt.

Each day, as the prince in him grew, the frog shrunk.

34

And the more <u>he</u> <u>saw</u> the princess in Libbie,

the more <u>she</u> <u>saw</u> what a wonderful princess she was.

35

Until
one night
as Princess Libbie kissed
Prince Freddie, the frog
shrunk and changed to
a golden frog, no larger
than a pin, deep in
Freddie's memory.

It was not a magical
kiss, although the kiss
felt magical.

36

It was the oh-so-short, yet so-very-long hours of sharing that changed Freddie into a Prince.

For Princess Libbie knew how to be a frog refiner.

One day,
Prince Freddie came by
with flowers and found
Princess Libbie in tears.

For the first
time, Freddie
saw <u>her</u> as a
frog.

But he
listened
patiently,
and tenderly
reminded her
of all her royal ways and
how she had
made a
prince
of him.

It did not happen in one great moment. But, gradually, over many days, her frog shrunk, until, as Freddie's had done, it became a golden glow in her memory.

For Freddie Frog
had learned to be a
frog refiner too.

As Freddie and Libbie
walked among the
princes and princesses,
they saw the golden
glows from within each
one, and walking among
the royal ones were the
frogs of the world...
all searching for a prince
or princess to give them
a golden glow.

And among the frogs they found an old friend, unnoticed before as they themselves grew.

Together, Freddie and Libbie began to seek for the gold and brought their friend into the royal family.

And the three began a quest...

for **YOU** and the royalty of the world.

OTHER OUTSTANDING
BOOKS FROM JALMAR PRESS

TA for TOTS (and other prinzes) $6.95

TA for KIDS (and grown-ups too) 4.95

TA for TEENS (and other important people) 7.95

The Original Warm Fuzzy Tale 3.95

TA for TOTS Coloring Book 1.95

TA for Management: Making Life Work 6.95

Joy of Backpacking: People's Guide
    to the Wilderness 5.95

A Time to Teach, A Time to Dance .... NOW 8.95

Reach for the Sky: The Romance and
    Technique of Hang-Gliding 7.95

The Parent Book: The Holistic Method for
    Raising the Emotionally Mature Child 9.95

Finding Hidden Treasure: TA Groups
    in the Church 6.95

Available from fine bookstores everywhere, or you may order directly from JALMAR PRESS, 650 Elvas Ave., Sacramento, CA 95819. Shipping and handling will be charged on all mail orders.